NORMAN
PRICE

BELLA
LASAGNE

JAMES

SARAH

MEET ALL THESE FRIENDS IN BUZZ BOOKS:

Thomas the Tank Engine
Fireman Sam
Looney Tunes
Tiny Toon Adventures
Bugs Bunny
Toucan 'Tecs
Flintstones
Jetsons
Joshua Jones

First published by Buzz Books,
an imprint of Reed Consumer Books Ltd
Michelin House, 81 Fulham Road, London SW3 6RB

LONDON MELBOURNE AUCKLAND

Based on the animation series produced by Bumper Films
for S4C/Channel 4 Wales and Prism Art & Design Ltd
Original idea by Dave Gingell and Dave Jones,
assisted by Mike Young. Characters created by Rob Lee.

ISBN 1 85591 252 X

Printed and bound in the UK by BPCC Hazell Books Ltd

ELVIS'S BIG DAY

Story by Rob Lee
Illustrations by The County Studio

Fireman Sam was in Dilys's shop buying his morning newspaper.

"Good morning, Dilys," he said. "How are you today?"

"Not so grand, Sam," Dilys replied. "I've got an awful headache."

"You should have a lie down," said Fireman Sam. "You'll feel much better."

"Sam's right," Dilys decided. "I'll close the shop for a little while and sneak upstairs for a snooze."

But on her way, Dilys remembered her laundry that was waiting to dry.

"More work," she sighed. She hung the wet clothes on the clothes horse and put it in front of the fire. "That laundry should be dry by the time I wake up."

Fireman Sam arrived at Pontypandy Fire Station just in time for breakfast.

"There are some very exotic recipes in this book," Elvis Cridlington remarked.

"Anything is more exotic than burnt bangers and cold beans," replied Trevor Evans, eyeing his plate warily.

Just then Station Officer Steele arrived with the morning post.

"Good news, Cridlington. You've passed your written examination for promotion."

"Congratulations, Elvis," said Sam.

"Now you're ready to take the practical part of the test, which we shall hold this afternoon," Station Officer Steele told Elvis. "The sooner the better, I always say."

"Er, yes, Sir," Elvis gulped. "The sooner the better."

That afternoon, Norman Price rushed home from school to find the shop closed.

"Mam must be sleeping," he thought as he tiptoed through the back door. "She wasn't very well this morning. I'll be extra quiet."

He noticed the clothes horse near the fire. "I'll just take my rugger shirt and be on my way. Mam knows I have a match today."

But as Norman grabbed his shirt, he accidentally knocked the clothes horse towards the open fire. He was in such a hurry to return to his game, he didn't notice the smoke rising toward the ceiling.

At the Fire Station, Elvis's practical examination was almost under way.

"Now then," said Station Officer Steele. "Firefighter Cridlington, your job will be to rescue Auxiliary Firefighter Evans from the roof of the training tower."

"The roof?" said Trevor in dismay. "But the only way to get to the roof is with a ladder."

"Exactly," said Station Officer Steele.

Carefully, Fireman Sam secured the ladder for Trevor.

"I don't like heights," muttered Trevor as he began climbing.

"Don't worry. Elvis will soon have you down on the ground again," said Sam.

"Are you ready, Firefighter Cridlington?" asked Station Officer Steele.

Elvis breathed deeply to calm his nerves. "Ready, Sir," he answered.

Station Officer Steele gave the signal, and Elvis quickly jumped out of Jupiter. Fireman Sam and Station Officer Steele were close behind.

Trevor was clinging to the railing around the roof. “Help! Help!” he cried.

“Take it easy, Trevor,” chuckled Fireman Sam. “This is only pretend.”

Elvis was taking the entire exercise very seriously. “Station Officer Steele and Fireman Sam, extend the triple extension ladder,” he ordered.

Down in the village, Sarah and James had stopped at Dilys's shop, only to find a CLOSED sign on the door.

"That's funny," said James. "I know that Norman is at his rugby match, but Mrs Price should be here."

"Let's try the back door," suggested Sarah.

But there was no answer at the back door either. The twins peered through the window into the lounge.

"Sarah, look!" James exclaimed. "Smoke!"

"And where there's smoke, there's fire!" cried Sarah. "Quickly, James, we'd better call the fire brigade!"

At the training tower, Elvis was just preparing to rescue Trevor when the alarm sounded.

"That's a real call out!" exclaimed Elvis.

Station Officer Steele read out the telex that had arrived at the station. "Fire at Mrs Price's shop," he said. "Let's go!"

The firefighters jumped into Jupiter, leaving Trevor stranded at the top of the training tower.

"Help! Get me down!" he shouted. "I'm afraid of heights!"

But Jupiter was already speeding off towards Pontypandy High Street.

As Jupiter raced into the High Street, the sound of the siren stirred Dilys.

"Oh dear, what a racket," she yawned. "There must be a fire in the village."

The siren seemed to be getting nearer. Dilys opened her eyes halfway. Was that smoke creeping into the bedroom? Suddenly Dilys jumped out of bed.

"Fire!" she screamed. "Help! Fire!"

Norman was on his way home from the rugby match when he saw Jupiter pull up outside the shop. Dilys was leaning out of the upstairs window.

"Guess what, Mam? We won our match!" called Norman.

"Stand back, Norman," said Station Officer Steele. "There's a fire!"

As the firefighters jumped out of Jupiter, Station Officer Steele said, "I'll start the hoses while Firefighter Cridlington rescues Mrs Price. Fireman Sam, you secure the ladder. Let's get a move on!"

Elvis beamed. This was his big chance! Quickly, he set up the double extension ladder and started climbing to the window. Suddenly, he wasn't nervous anymore. After all, he was Firefighter Elvis Cridlington.

"Don't worry, Dilys," he said confidently. "I know exactly what to do."

Elvis helped Dilys out of the window and onto his shoulder in the firefighter's lift. Slowly and carefully, he made his way to the ground.

Firefighter Penny Morris arrived at Pontypandy Fire Station from Newtown to find that no one was there. She was about to drive away in Venus, her rescue tender, when she heard a shout. She decided to investigate.

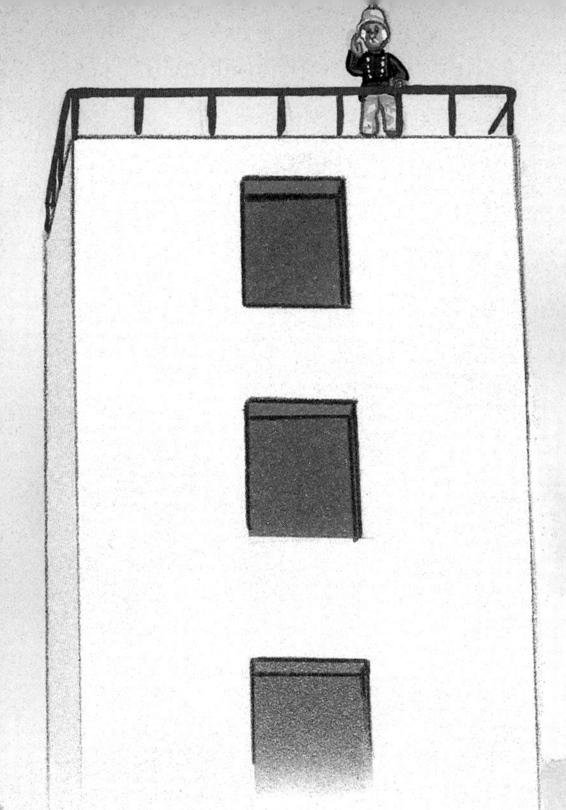

"Penny, help!" Trevor cried from the top of the training tower.

Penny looked up. "Trevor, what on earth are you doing up there?"

"I'll tell you as soon as you help me down," called Trevor.

"Don't worry, Trevor," she called back. "I'll have you down in no time."

At Dilys's shop, the fire brigade quickly extinguished the fire.

"You must always keep a guard on an open fire," Elvis told Dilys, "and *never* put a clothes horse in front of the fire."

"Quite right, Cridlington," said Station Officer Steele. "Excellent job today, in fact."

"Thank you, Sir," said Elvis proudly.

Just then Venus arrived at the shop.

"Have you forgotten someone?" Penny asked with a smile.

"Trevor!" Elvis exclaimed.

"Yes, thanks to Penny, here I am," said Trevor. "I'm afraid you'll have to rescue someone else for your practical, Elvis."

"He already has," said Station Officer Steele. "Elvis, I was about to tell you that you've passed the promotion exam."

Elvis's smile spread right across his face as everyone congratulated him.

That evening, Elvis cooked one of the exotic recipes from his new book. “Stewed dumplings and pickled mustard greens,” he said proudly. “Looks delicious, doesn't it?”

“Er, interesting, Elvis,” said Trevor.

“Now that you’ve been promoted, you needn’t be our mess officer, Firefighter Cridlington,” said Station Officer Steele.

“But I like cooking,” Elvis protested.

“Yes, well, I suppose you may continue as the mess officer, if you'd like,” said Station Officer Steele.

“Thank you, Sir,” said Elvis. “In fact, I've already chosen a recipe for tomorrow's tea — beetroot and baked bean casserole.”

"I can't wait,” chuckled Fireman Sam.

FIREMAN SAM

STATION OFFICER
STEELE

TREVOR EVANS

ELVIS
CRIDLINGTON

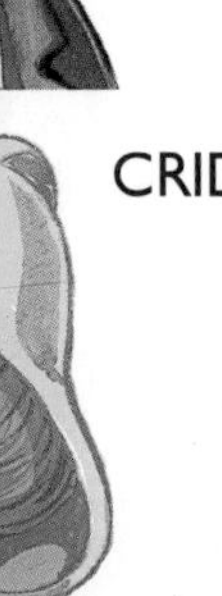

PENNY MORRIS